## A Note from Michelle about
# My Super Sleepover Book

Hi! I'm Michelle Tanner. I'm nine years old, and I just love sleepover parties. How about you? It's fun to party and spend the night with friends. It's even more fun to wake up in the morning and have breakfast together!

*My Super Sleepover Book* is a special present from me to you—to help you have the best sleepover ever. It's packed full of super party ideas. Like how to camp out inside. And how to create great makeover magic. There's lots more stuff, too. It's guaranteed by ME to be special fun for YOU!

I'll help you choose party themes, invitations, food for supper, snacks, and breakfast treats. I'll share my special tips for super-fun party games, craft activities, and even party favors that are fun to make at home and *more* fun to take home!

Read through all my party ideas. Then pick the party you want to plan first. Are you ready for your Super Sleepover? On your mark, get set, PARTY!

# FULL HOUSE™ MICHELLE novels

The Great Pet Project
The Super-Duper Sleepover Party
My Two Best Friends
Lucky, Lucky Day
The Ghost in My Closet
Ballet Surprise
Major League Trouble
My Fourth-Grade Mess
Bunk 3, Teddy and Me
My Best Friend Is a Movie Star! (Super Special)
The Big Turkey Escape
The Substitute Teacher
Calling All Planets
I've Got a Secret
How to Be Cool
The Not-So-Great Outdoors
My Ho-Ho-Horrible Christmas
My Almost Perfect Plan
April Fools!
My Life Is a Three-Ring Circus
Welcome to My Zoo
The Problem with Pen Pals
Tap Dance Trouble

**Activity Books**
My Awesome Holiday Friendship Book
My Super Sleepover Book

Available from MINSTREL Books

# FULL HOUSE™
# Michelle

## My Super Sleepover Book

### Linda Williams Aber

A Parachute Book

A MINSTREL® BOOK

Published by POCKET BOOKS
New York   London   Toronto   Sydney   Tokyo   Singapore

A MINSTREL PAPERBACK *Original*

A Minstrel Book published by
POCKET BOOKS, a division of Simon & Schuster Inc.
1230 Avenue of the Americas, New York, NY 10020

A PARACHUTE BOOK

Copyright © and ™ 1999 by Warner Bros.

FULL HOUSE, characters, names and all related indicia are trademarks of Warner Bros. © 1999.

ISBN: 0-671-02701-8

First Minstrel Books printing February 1999

10  9  8  7  6  5  4  3  2  1

A MINSTREL BOOK and colophon are registered trademarks of Simon & Schuster Inc.

Cover photo by Schultz Photography

Printed in the U.S.A.

# Contents

# My Super
# Sleepover Book

# Introduction

## Michelle's Special Invitation

Hi! I'm Michelle Tanner. I'm nine years old. And I think sleepover parties are totally awesome! It's so cool to get your friends together for a night of pillow fights, popcorn, and fun. And it's even *cooler* if your party has a theme.

So grab your sleeping bag and get ready to stay up all night. I'm inviting you and your friends to see how I make my sleepover parties *super!*

Who do you want to come?

_____

(Write your name here.)

_____

(Write your friend's name here.)

_____

(Write your friend's name here.)

_____

(Write your friend's name here.)

_____

(Write your friend's name here.)

_____

(Write your friend's name here.)

What kind of sleepover party do you want to have? I've got lots of ideas. How about camping indoors or pretending that you and your friends are movie stars? Maybe you could have a scary sleepover or a magic sleepover. An evening of silly Olympics events is fun, too. You and your friends might even want to spend the night being super-models.

All you have to do is pick a theme and you're on your way to having the most super sleepover ever.

So, come on. Let's party!

# Michelle's Best Bets for Goodie Bags and Keepsakes

You don't have to spend a lot of money to give your sleepover party guests really cool stuff!

**When sleepover guests arrive, start the fun by giving out one or two of these items. It's the thought that counts, and these thoughts are cool!**

- ♥ new toothbrush and mini-tube of toothpaste
- ♥ mini-flashlight
- ♥ scrunchie bands and barrettes
- ♥ pocket mirror

- ♥ pocket hairbrush
- ♥ sleep mask (to cover eyes and keep the light out)
- ♥ mini–stuffed animal
- ♥ bottle of water with friend's name on it
- ♥ mini-shampoo/conditioner
- ♥ individual soap

**When the party is over, these items make a goodie bag great!**

- ★ make-your-own friendship bracelet strings
- ★ stick-on earrings
- ★ fake tattoos
- ★ glitter stickers
- ★ mini–address book
- ★ cool key chains
- ★ diary or journal
- ★ pens, pencils, and markers
- ★ mini–photo album
- ★ autograph book

## Pick a Party!

You've already decided to have a Super Sleepover party. That's terrific! But which one should you try first? I always have a theme. Here are my six favorite Super Sleepover ideas. They are all different, but one thing about them is the same—they're tons of FUN!

Party 1:   Camp-out Sleep-in Sleepover
Party 2:   Fabulously Famous Sleepover
Party 3:   Completely Creepy Sleepover
Party 4:   Seriously Silly Olympics Sleepover
Party 5:   Abracadabra Super Magic Sleepover
Party 6:   Supermodel Makeover Sleepover

# Party 1: Camp-out Sleep-in Sleepover

Roll up the tent flaps. Roll in the camp cots. And roll out the red carpet to all your camp-out friends! Rain or shine, this super sleepover party brings the fun inside. So pitch your tent and get ready to be a very happy camper!

## In-Tents Invitations!

Creating your own invitations makes your party special right from the start. Wait till your friends receive their tent-shaped invitations. They'll know your Camp-out Sleep-in Sleepover party will be tent-loads of fun.

6

*You will need:*

✂ 8½-by-11-inch colored construction paper, ½ sheet for each invitation
✂ scissors
✂ pen

Lay the paper on a flat surface. Fold the top two corners down so that they meet in the middle of the paper. It will look like a triangle or a tent. Cut off the extra paper along the bottom of the tent. Then, using that paper, repeat the instructions. Now you have two tent invitations. Open the tent flaps. Your invitations should look like this:

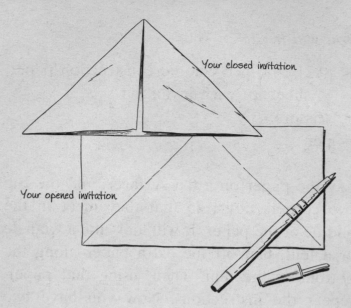

Your closed invitation

Your opened invitation

Write the following information inside each invitation:

You're invited to a Camp-out Sleep-in Sleep-over party!

Come sleep over at＿＿＿＿＿＿＿'s house!

Address:＿＿＿＿＿＿＿＿＿＿＿＿＿＿＿

Date:＿＿＿＿＿＿＿ Time:＿＿＿＿＿＿

Pickup time next morning:＿＿＿＿＿＿＿

RSVP＿＿＿＿＿＿＿＿＿＿＿＿＿＿＿＿＿

## Outside-In Decorations

Bring nature inside to set the scene for a cozy night. Set up your tents around a flashlight campfire, under a starry-night sky. It's easy! Just follow the directions below:

*For each tent you will need:*

- one blanket or sheet
- two chairs
- one long rope or cord
- several books or other heavy objects

Place two chairs opposite each other about five feet apart. Tie the rope or cord between the tops of the two chairs. Carefully hang the blanket or sheet over the rope. Spread the sides of the blanket and place books or other heavy objects on the ends to hold the blanket in place. Make each tent big enough for two sleeping bags.

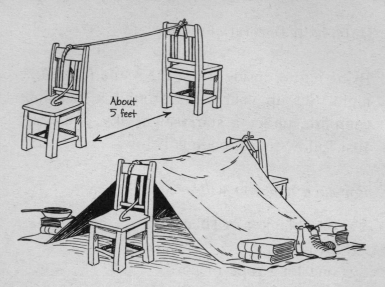

About
5 feet

*Now create your starry-night sky. You will
need:*

★ six sheets of poster board
★ a star-shaped cookie cutter or cardboard
  star-shaped pattern
★ aluminum foil
★ scissors
★ hole punch
★ string
★ clear tape

Place the cookie cutter or star-shaped pattern
on the poster board. Trace around the shape.

10

Make as many stars as you want. Cut out the stars. Cover them with aluminum foil. Punch a hole in one point of each star and tie a long string through each hole. Ask an adult to help you tape the strings to the ceiling.

*Now make a flashlight campfire the centerpiece of your party room. You will need:*

★ six brown paper bags
★ tape
★ two flashlights

Roll up each bag in the shape of a log, starting at the open edge and rolling tightly. Tape the edges to hold the shape.

Place the flashlights on the floor where your campfire will be. Lean the paper logs against each other to form a teepee around the flashlights. Turn the flashlights on. Turn out the lights in the room. Adjust the flashlights so that your campfire glows just the way you want it to.

# Camp-out Sleep-in Activities

## Stupid Fishing Tricks

No worms. No hooks. No kidding! Here's a fishing game that's fun. Even for friends who squirm at the sight of a worm. Fish for these balloons filled with funny things to do. Prepare the fish pond ahead of time. Then catch lots of laughs at your party!

*You will need:*

- writing paper
- balloons
- strings
- a big cardboard box

Cut the piece of paper into strips long enough to hold a short message. Write a message on each strip. Here are some sample messages you can use:

- Stick out your tongue and say "Aahhh!"
- Pretend to sneeze ten times in a row.

13

- Laugh and don't stop until everyone else is laughing, too.
- Sing "Row, Row, Row Your Boat" as loud as you can.
- Jump up and down and shout, "A bug! A bug! A bug!"
- Throw kisses to everyone as you say, "Thank you! Thank you! Thank you!"
- Flap your arms up and down as if you are flying.
- Stick your thumbs in your ears, wiggle your fingers, and make a funny face.

Roll the messages up. Stuff one inside each balloon. Blow up the balloons and tie the ends. Then tie a string to each balloon. Put the balloons in the cardboard box. Leave the strings hanging over the side. Twist the strings together.

Let everyone grab a loose end and follow the string till it reaches a balloon. Each camper should step on it, sit on it, or squeeze it until it pops. Then they must read their message and do whatever it says!

Some of the funniest stories are the ones that seem to go on forever. Here's one never-ending story you can tell around your flashlight campfire:

**It was a dark, dark night on a high, high hill. There were ten girls sitting around a campfire. One said, "(say** name of guest to the left)**! Tell us a story!"**

**So** (say name of guest to the left) **began:** (The guest to the left starts the story all over again!)

**It was a dark, dark night on a high, high hill. There were ten girls sitting around a campfire. One said, "(say** name of guest to the left)**! Tell us a story!"**

**So** (say name of guest to the left) **began: It was a dark, dark night . . .** and so on.

Repeat until every guest has had a turn to tell the story twice—or until someone yells, "STOP! Please!"

Sit around your campfire, holding a flashlight under your chin. Point it up at your face as you start telling one of the tales of terror below. Then pass the flashlight to the girl on your left. She adds one or two more lines to the story and passes the flashlight to the next girl. Each person in the circle adds one or two more lines to the story. Keep the story going as long as possible. The one who finally ends the tale has to begin the *next* one! Here are some sample tales of terror to get your game started:

📖 You're not going to believe what I am about to tell you, but it's all true. On my way over here tonight, I heard a kitten crying. But when I looked behind the bushes, I couldn't believe my own eyes! There was a . . .

📖 Sometimes my own lunch scares me. The other day I brought my lunch to school in a paper bag. When I reached into the bag to get my sandwich,

16

something furry touched my hand! I screamed and then I . . .

Once upon a time, a long time ago, there was a group of kids just like us. They were all sitting around a campfire just like this one. Suddenly one of the girls started . . .

# Super Campsite Supper

Spread out a picnic blanket on the floor and serve up a genuine camp-out meal! Make up some camp-themed names for your food and write them on index cards. Then place the cards in front of each dish.

## Some Camp-out Supper Suggestions Are:

★ Hot dogs in buns (Label them "Dogs-in-a-Blanket")
★ Hamburgers on buns (Label them "Trail Blazer Burgers")
★ Chips and dips (Label them "Trail Snacks")
★ Carrot sticks and celery sticks (Label them "Nature's Bounty")
★ Pink lemonade (Label it "Camp-out Quencher")

18

## For Dessert Try This Super Idea for Chocolate Big Dippers!

*You will need:*

★ marshmallows
★ strawberries
★ apples cut into bite-size pieces
★ pineapple chunks
★ bottled chocolate sauce
★ forks

Set out bowls of marshmallows, strawberries, apple pieces, and pineapple chunks. Fill a big bowl with chocolate sauce. Give each guest a fork. Spear a marshmallow or piece of fresh fruit with your fork and dip it into the sauce for Big Dipper fun!

## Starry-Night Snack Attack

When the midnight munchies strike, pass out individual plastic bags of popcorn that you've made ahead of time.

19

## Sunup Eat-in Breakfast

Roll up the sleeping bags! Pack up the tents! And hike on over to the kitchen for breakfast. Offer a selection of cereals, juices, and milk. A simple breakfast after a long night of camping out is definitely the *in* thing to do!

# Party 2: Fabulously Famous Sleepover

Congratulations! You and all your friends are about to be famous! Invite everyone to come to your party dressed as their favorite movie or music star. Try to guess who's who at your sleepover. And remember to take a fabulously famous photo of everyone in her star-studded best!

## Fabulously Famous Invitations

Your friends will love these invitations—they look just like movie tickets! Your Fabulously

Famous Sleepover party invitations will remind everyone that it's a costume party. They'll have fun dressing up like famous celebrities.

*You will need:*

✂ colored construction paper
✂ black marker
✂ scissors

Cut a piece of construction paper in half lengthwise. Draw a border in the shape of a ticket as in the sample below. Write "ADMIT ONE" across the top of the ticket. Then fill in the rest of the important facts about your party. Your invitation should look like this:

---

### ADMIT ONE
To a Fabulously Famous Sleepover Party at
_____ 's house!

Address: _____

Date: _____ Time: _____

Pickup time next morning: _____

It's a costume party—dress up like your favorite celebrity!

Bring a sleeping bag and your sleepover stuff!

RSVP _____

---

## Set the Scene

Make your party room cozy with piles of pillows and stuffed animals. Now sit back and discuss the best things about being famous!

*For your Fabulously Famous decorations you will need:*

★ posters and magazine pictures of famous people
★ crepe paper streamers
★ balloons
★ glitter glue
★ clear tape
★ scissors
★ string

Hang posters of famous movie and music stars—past and present—on the walls of your party room. Cut out pictures of celebrities from magazines and paste them onto construction paper. Tape them to the walls, too. Then drape crepe paper streamers on the walls around the room.

Blow up a balloon and tie the end. Hold the balloon by the end. Using the glitter glue, draw a big star on it. Repeat for all the balloons. After the balloons are dry, tie a length of string to each balloon. Have an adult help you tape them to the ceiling and in doorways. And when your guests walk into your party room, they'll know they're really partying with the stars!

# Games of the Fabulously Famous

Ever wonder what it would be like to be a famous star? Here's your chance to find out! You and your friends will have a ball dressing up and acting like your favorite TV, movie, and music stars at this glamour-filled, fun-filled sleepover! Remember to smile—because the spotlight is on you!

## Autographs, Please!

Get your party off to a famous start with this face-to-face-with-the-famous game.

*For this game you will need:*

- white pillowcases
- fabric markers

First supply each guest with a plain white pillowcase and a fabric marker. Then have each guest try to guess who the other famous guests are. When the giggling stops, have everyone sign each other's pillowcase with

25

their real names and the names of the famous people they're dressed to look like. For example a guest might write:

> To Shirley Temple (Mandy Metz)
> I'll always remember when we met at this fabulous party for the famous!
> > Your friend forever,
> > Pocahontas (Michelle Tanner)

And the autographed pillowcase makes a perfect favor from your sleepover party!

## Totally Weird Talent Test

It's time to see who's got star talent! Find out with this fabulously funny game!

*For this game you will need:*

- pillowcase
- paper
- marker

Before your party, write directions on slips of paper. Fold the papers and put them into a

26

pillowcase. When it's time to play the game, turn off all the lights and let a spotlight (or a flashlight) shine on your stars! Now have each guest pick out a piece of paper, and follow the directions.

Here are some ideas for things to write on the papers. Don't forget to add some ideas of your own!

☆ You have one line in a new movie. Practice saying it six different ways. The line is: "Don't you dare laugh at me!"

☆ You're in a *silent* movie. Your part calls for a horrifying scream! Face your audience. Look horrified and scream— without sound, of course!

☆ You're the star of a new musical. Too bad you have a terrible cold. Because the show must go on. You must sing "Twinkle, Twinkle, Little Star." Sing it while you hold your nose so you sound as if you have a cold.

☆ You are trying out for a part in a television

commercial, selling a new laundry soap called Slime. Hold up a box of Slime and convince your audience that Slime cleans clothes better than ordinary soap.

☆ You have to try out for a play, but you just got the hiccups! Here's the line you have to say. Hiccup after each word in the line: "I (hiccup) think (hiccup) people (hiccup) who (hiccup) hiccup (hiccup) in (hiccup) public (hiccup) are (hiccup) so (hiccup) rude! (hiccup) Don't (hiccup) you? (hiccup)

## Gossip Column

Ever wonder how rumors get started in Hollywood newspaper gossip columns? See for yourself how the gossip game works.

Turn the lights off and arrange your sleeping bags in a circle. Whisper to the person next to you something like, "Six slick flick stars flicked six trick fleas far." Make sure no one else can hear you. Then say, "Pass it on."

The second player must then whisper the rumor to the next person. Keep the gossip going to the next person and the next—until everyone in the circle has heard it. The last person must then say out loud what she thinks she has heard. You'll be surprised at what comes out!

Try these other rumors. Then make up one or two of your own!

"Most movie lovers go out at night only to world premieres."

"The biggest star I ever saw was a famous dog named Bo-Bo."

This is how lots of rumors—and lots of laughs—get started!

# Fabulously Famous Supper

You'll treat your guests like stars when you serve this Academy Award–winning buffet! Set the table ahead of time with plates, utensils, and napkins at one end. Arrange platters of food on the rest of the table. And make up some fabulously funny names for the food you'll be serving.

## Some Fabulously Famous Supper Suggestions Are:

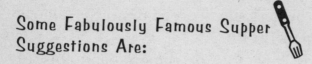

● "Starring Rolls" and "Make-Your-Own Heroes"
Pile a plate high with sandwich rolls. Set out dishes of sandwich fixings such as turkey, ham, bologna, cheese, lettuce, tomatoes, mayonnaise, mustard, and pickles. Add bowls of fruit salad, pasta salad, and garden salad.

♥ "Celebrity Sweetshakes"

*For this fabulously famous drink you will need:*

♥ 1 quart of ginger ale
♥ 1 large can frozen orange juice concentrate (mixed according to the directions on the can)
♥ 1 pint of orange sherbet
♥ 1 pint of lemon sherbet

In a large punch bowl, mixing bowl, or big kitchen pot, mix ginger ale and juice together. Use a sherbet scoop or large spoon to scoop out balls of sherbet. Float the sherbet balls in the punch.

♥ "Famous Faces Cupcakes"
Serve your guests cupcakes with icing on top. With an adult's help, use decorating icing to create celebrity faces on the cupcakes. Add icing hair, earrings, and hair ribbons. Then have your guests guess who each cupcake is supposed to be. You'll be famous for these for sure!

## Midnight Snack

When the clock strikes twelve or whenever hunger strikes, ask an adult to help you with this easy-to-make snack-attack tackler. Cover a microwave-safe plate with tortilla chips. Sprinkle the chips with shredded cheddar cheese. Microwave on high for 40 seconds.

## Breakfast Productions Presents . . . Gone with the Waffles!

Make your breakfast for the stars a fabulously famous production. Your guests don't need to wear costumes in the morning. But that doesn't mean the waffles you serve can't be dressed up!

With an adult's help, prepare frozen waffles in the toaster oven. Serve them with a choice of toppings: jellies and jams, fresh fruit, syrup, and powdered sugar.

Offer pitchers of cold milk and juice. It's the perfect way to end your party, and start your guests off to a fabulous day!

# Party 3: Completely Creepy Sleepover

You don't have to wait for Halloween to have a Completely Creepy Sleepover party. Invite the "ghouls" over for a howling good time in your creepy "hall of horrors." It's all for fun, of course. And your guests will get a laugh and a half out of this icky, yucky, Completely Creepy Sleepover!

## Completely Creepy Invitations!

Your friends will get the creeps as soon as they receive your bat-shaped invitation. Soon they'll be hanging around for a frightfully fun night of games, food, and sleepover scares.

*You will need:*

✂ 8½-by-11-inch cardboard
✂ 8½-by-11-inch black construction paper, ½ sheet for each invitation
✂ plain white paper, ½ sheet for each invitation
✂ scissors
✂ pen
✂ tape or glue stick

Draw an outline of a bat with its wings open on the cardboard. The bat should be big enough to fit on ½ sheet of construction paper. Cut out the bat shape to make a pattern. Trace a bat shape onto several pieces of black construction paper. Cut out the bats. (See the sample below.)

*Pssst!* You're invited to a **Completely Creepy Sleepover Party!** Don't be scared! It's all for fun! Bring your sleeping bag and your overnight stuff to _____ 's house!
Address: _____
Date: _____
Time: _____ Pickup time next morning: _____
RSVP _____

Now cut out squares of white paper small enough to fit in the middle of each bat shape. Glue or tape the paper onto the bats. Write this party information on the paper:

Psssst! You're invited to a Completely Creepy Sleepover party!

Don't be scared! It's all for fun! Bring your sleeping bag and your overnight stuff to ____ _____' s house!

Address:_____

Date:_____ Time:_____

Pickup time next morning:_____

RSVP_____

## "Hall of Horrors" Decorations

Your guests will get the creeps and the giggles when they crawl through the crepe paper "cave entrance" to your "hall of horrors." With an adult's help, put night-lights in every electrical outlet. Then ask an adult to change

35

the regular lightbulbs in the lamps around the room to blue or red ones. Now switch on the lights and get ready for some ghoulish foolishness!

*For your "hall of horrors" you will need:*

- black and purple crepe paper streamers
- black pipe cleaners
- cardboard boxes
- gray and black paint
- paintbrushes
- bat pattern from your Completely Creepy invitations
- black construction paper
- old newspapers
- white plastic garbage bags
- string
- clear tape
- scissors

Create the creepy cave entrance to the party room by taping long black and purple streamers from the top of the doorway so they dangle to the floor. Ask an adult to help you. Your guests will have to push the streamers

36

aside to enter. Hang streamers over the windows, too.

Then dangle pipe-cleaner spiders from the ceiling. To make a spider, place one pipe cleaner on top of another—so that they make an X (or four spider legs). Twist the top pipe cleaner once around the bottom one (It should still look like an X). Twist two more pipe cleaners around the center of the X. Now you have eight "legs" sticking out. Bend each leg from the middle to make your spider stand. Make as many spiders as you like. Tie different lengths of string around each spider. Tape them to the ceiling.

Trace the bat pattern on black construction paper. Cut out bats. Then hang the creepy creatures around the room.

Using big cardboard boxes from the grocery store, cut out tombstone shapes. Paint them gray. When they're dry, paint "R.I.P." on each in big black letters. Write the name of each guest on a tombstone, too. Lean the tombstones against the walls, or tape them to the back of each chair at the dinner table.

Crumple up a few sheets of newspaper.

Form into several balls the size of a human head. Put one head in each white trash bag. Tie it just under the ball so the bag looks like a ghost! Hang ghosts around the party room.

Congratulations! Your party room looks BOO-tiful!

# Ghoulish Games

Everyone likes to be scared—when it's only for fun. Your sleepover wouldn't be completely creepy without playing some frightfully funny party games. So bring on the spiders, snakes, and werewolves. You'll soon be howling with laughter!

## I Spy Spiders

*For this game you will need:*

* 🕷 10 plastic or pipe-cleaner spiders
* 🕷 paper
* 🕷 pens

Before the party begins, mark 10 plastic or pipe-cleaner spiders with a number from 1 to 10. Place the spiders around the party room in hard-to-see and obvious places. When it's time to play the game, give each guest a paper and pencil and have them walk around the room looking for spiders. As they find spiders, they should write down the numbers. (Don't move the spiders!) The first guest to write down all 10 spider numbers wins!

## Who's Afraid of the Big Bad Werewolf?

How well do you know your sleepover friends? Here's a game that will tell you everything you need to know about who's afraid of what!

*For this game you will need:*

 paper
pencils
pillowcase

Arrange your sleeping bags in a circle. Give each friend a slip of paper and a pencil. Have each guest write down the things that give her the creeps. Don't show one another the papers. When everyone has written down at least three creepy things, put all the papers into a pillowcase. Pass the pillowcase around the circle. Take turns reaching in and taking out a piece of paper. Read the creepy list out loud. Then everyone must try to guess whose list it is!

## Make a Snake and Eat It!

*For this game you will need:*

- O-shaped cereal (such as Cheerios or Froot Loops)
- bowls
- string
- timer

Give each player a bowl full of O-shaped cereal and a 24-inch-long piece of string. Set a timer for two minutes. At the word "Go!" everyone must start stringing the cereal. When the timer bell rings, everyone must stop stringing. Check to see who made the longest snake. The girl with the longest snake will think she won the game—until she finds out that now it's time to eat the snake! At the word "Eat!" everyone must gobble down the snake she made. The one who finishes first wins!

41

## Paint a Creepy Pumpkin

If your party is scheduled around Halloween time, set out pumpkins, acrylic paints, and paintbrushes. Give each guest her own pumpkin to paint. Anything goes! Faces, polka dots, stripes, or patterns. Then have a pumpkin autograph session. Pass the pumpkins around for each guest to sign, just for fun. Now everyone has a souvenir to take home.

# Scary (and Delicious!) Supper

Create a feast fit for a beast! Cover your table with black paper. Make funny labels for each platter of food, and place them in front of each dish. Then let your ghoul-friends serve themselves.

## Some Scary Supper Suggestions Are:

★ Spaghetti with sauce (Label it "Wiggly-Worms")
★ Salad (Label it "Ghastly Greens")
★ Italian bread (Label it "Crusty Stuff")
★ Chocolate milk (Label it "Swamp Swill")

## And for Dessert, Your Guests Can Make Their Own Ice *Scream* Sandwiches!

*You Will Need:*

★ graham crackers
★ ice cream in brick form
★ chocolate chips

Open the ice cream box completely so that it may be sliced easily. Ask an adult to cut the ice cream small enough to fit between graham crackers. Sandwich the ice cream slices between two graham crackers. Pour some chocolate chips onto a plate. Then roll the ice cream sides of the sandwich in the chips to decorate. If you wish to make these ahead of time, wrap them in foil or plastic wrap and store them in the freezer until serving time.

## Midnight Snack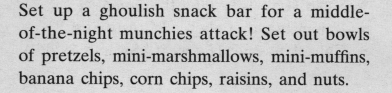

Set up a ghoulish snack bar for a middle-of-the-night munchies attack! Set out bowls of pretzels, mini-marshmallows, mini-muffins, banana chips, corn chips, raisins, and nuts.

## Shrunken-Head Coffin Cakes

Good morning! It's time for your ghoul-friends to roll out of their coffins and into the kitchen for surprising shrunken-head pancakes! Use raisins or mini–chocolate bits to make eyes, noses, and ghoulishy grinning mouths on each teeny-weenie cake.

You and your guests can mix the pancake batter. Then ask an adult to help you drop the batter onto the griddle. Make cakes the size of a silver dollar and pile them high! You might also drizzle on fruit-flavored syrup. Either way, get ready for big giggles. Serve plenty of juice to wash the pancakes down.

When your coffin cakes are gone, give a big thanks to all your friends for coming to your Completely Creepy Sleepover party!

# Party 4: Seriously Silly Olympics Sleepover

You don't have to be a great athlete to have a ball at your Seriously Silly Olympics Sleepover. It's the gold-medal-winning, giggle-getting event of the year! Let your friends be the judges. They're sure to give this sleepover party a perfect score!

## Gold Medal Invitations

When their gold medal invitations arrive, your friends will know this party is a real winner!

*You will need:*

✄ 8½-by-11-inch yellow construction paper
✄ A small plate, six inches across
✄ pen
✄ scissors
✄ hole punch
✄ yellow ribbon

For each invitation, place the plate in the center of the paper. Trace around it. Cut out the circle. Write this party information on the medal:

Be a sport! Come to a
Seriously Silly Olympics Sleepover
Games! Prizes! Food! Fun!

Date: _____

Time: _____

Place: _____

Pickup time next morning:_____

Bring a sleeping bag and your overnight things.

RSVP _____

Now punch a hole at the top of the circle. Thread yellow ribbon through the hole and tie it at the ends to make your invitation a necklace with a gold medal pendant. It should look like this:

## It's a Weird, Weird Olympics World!

**BE A SPORT!**
Come to a
Seriously Silly Olympics Sleepover!
Games! Prizes! Food! Fun!

Date: _____

Time: _____

Place: _____

Pickup time next morning: _____

Bring a sleeping bag and your overnight things.

RSVP _____

Silly signs, made-up medals, and funny flags of all nations set the scene for your silly Olympics party room. There's not a rink, track, court, slope, balance beam, or mat in sight. Because this competition is for seriously silly sports only!

*You will need:*

🎗 colored construction paper and poster paper
🎗 pen
🎗 scissors

48

🎗 colored marking pens
🎗 hole punch
🎗 string
🎗 tape

## Seriously Silly Signs

Here are some ideas for seriously silly signs to hang around your party room:

✎ Speed Eating Competition
✎ Downhill Rolling-in-a-Sleeping Bag Competition
✎ Snoring Competition
✎ Synchronized Sleeping
✎ This Way to the Stadium (with arrows going all ways)

Make up some other signs using your own funny ideas.

## Funny Flags

Design your own Olympic flags. Make up silly nations and silly sayings for each one.

Here are some of my favorite ideas:

- United States of Party Animals—Party Hardy
- The Nation of Hungry—In Midnight Snacks We Trust
- The Nation of Grease—George Washington Slipped Here!

## Made-up Medals

Using the directions for creating your Seriously Silly Olympics invitations, make more gold medals to hang around your party room. Here are some ideas for what to write on the medals:

- 1st Place in Snoring
- Champion Sleeper
- Gold Medal Snacker
- 1st Place in Giggling

While you are making medals for decorations, make plenty of extra medals, too. You'll need them later for the winners of each party game! To make them special, tape a piece of your favorite wrapped hard candy to the center of each medal.

## Games Galore That Are Sure to Score

You're sure to win the gold for organizing the goofiest Olympics ever! Hand out medals to all your guests. Because at these games, everyone's a winner!

## Stomach Slalom Ski Race

In this race, you ski on your stomach instead of a mountain! Pick a place to start the race. Set up a finish line. Have two girls stretch out on their tummies inside their sleeping bags at the starting line. On the word "Go!" the two racers must inch their way toward the finish line in their sleeping bags. Using hands is allowed. After each pair of racers has raced, the winners in each pair will race against each other. Keep racing until there is only one winner left.

## Last Laps Event

She who laps last, laps best! The point of this game is to sit as many people in a chair as possible. The first person sits in a chair. The second sitter sits in the first person's lap. Add a third, fourth, fifth—as many as you can. (Invite siblings to join in this game just to add more laps.) The more the merrier! Everyone's a medal winner in this laps-for-laughs game!

## Easy-Knee-Z Relay Event

Two beach balls, two books, and two teams make this relay game too funny for words!

The two teams line up behind a starting line. The first player in each line starts the race with a beach ball squeezed between her knees and a book balanced on her head. On the word "Go!" they both race to the finish line. If the book or ball is dropped, that player must go back to the starting line.

After a player reaches the finish line, she carries the ball and book back to her team, and hands them over to the next player in line. The first team to finish the relay wins!

### Hit-the-Sack Sack Race

Let your sleeping bags be the sacks. Players stand in their sleeping bag sacks, holding them up to their waists with their hands. On the word "Go!" players hop toward a finish line. The first one over the line bags a medal!

### Last-Licks Event

Single-stick Popsicles make this the tastiest game ever! All players are given a Popsicle. On the word "Go!" the licking begins! No biting or chewing allowed! The first player to get down to the stick wins a medal—lickety-split!

# The Seriously Silly Olympics Supper Wrap-Up

When the games are over, it's time for the big wrap-up! No, the party isn't wrapping up. The supper is! Let your champs chomp on delicious wrap sandwiches they make themselves. Then you can all be the judges and decide which wrap is the best!

*For your Seriously Silly Olympics wraps you will need:*

- ♥ aluminum foil squares
- ♥ soft flour tortillas
- ♥ deli cold cuts (bologna, turkey, salami, Swiss cheese)
- ♥ tuna fish salad
- ♥ egg salad
- ♥ shredded lettuce
- ♥ shredded cheese
- ♥ chopped tomatoes/salsa
- ♥ mayonnaise, relish, mustard, sour cream, guacamole

Lay the tortilla on a piece of foil. Add your choice of fillings and fold up the bottom half of the tortilla. Roll up the tortilla. Then wrap the foil around it. The foil will hold the sandwich closed.

## For Dessert, Serve Winter Olympics Ice Cream Snowballs

*You will need:*

* ❄ ice cream scoop
* ❄ ice cream
* ❄ toppings such as coconut, chocolate sprinkles, colored sprinkles, crumbled Oreos, crushed chocolate bars, chopped nuts

Scoop out ice cream balls ahead of time. Wrap each ball in plastic. Keep them in the freezer. When it's time for dessert, set out bowls of toppings and a big bowl of frozen ice cream balls. Let each guest roll the ice cream balls in the toppings of her choice.

## Seriously Sporty Midnight Snacks

A light snack is what Olympic champions choose after an evening filled with serious sporting events. Set out a plate filled with apple slices, orange sections, and grapes. Add bowls of corn chips, sunflower seeds, and raisins. These snacks will score big for sure!

## Breakfast of Champions!

Breakfast is the final event of your Seriously Silly Olympics Sleepover. Award your winning crowd with these tasty treats.

### Long-Jump Juice Pops

*You will need:*

* small paper cups
* cookie sheet
* fruit juice (any kind)
* aluminum foil
* scissors
* spoons or Popsicle sticks

These juicy breakfast pops will have you jumping for joy. Make them the day before your party.

Place cups on a cookie sheet—one cup for each guest. Then pour your favorite fruit juice into each. Don't fill the cups to the very top.

Cover each cup with aluminum foil. Poke a hole in the center of each piece of foil. Stick a spoon handle or Popsicle stick through the hole and into the cup. The foil will keep the handle standing up straight until the juice freezes. Freeze for at least two hours.

To remove the frozen pop from the cup, run a little warm water over the outside of the cup.

## Mini-Marathon Morning Pizzas

Everyone loves pizza. This breakfast version will give you energy to last all day long!

*You will need:*

- bagels or English muffins
- toppings such as peanut butter and jelly, honey and shredded coconut
- toaster oven

Split the bagels or English muffins into halves. With the help of an adult, toast them in the toaster oven until lightly browned.

Spread peanut butter and jelly or honey and shredded coconut on the bagels or muffins. Put them on the toaster oven pan insert. Set the pan back into the toaster oven. Leave in for two minutes.

Have an adult use pot holders to remove the pan from the toaster oven. Let the minipizzas cool for a few minutes before eating. No racing to finish first!

When the party is over, your winning feelings will remain if you say thanks to everyone for helping you have a Seriously Silly Olympics Sleepover!

# Party 5: Abracadabra Super Magic Sleepover

Treat your friends to a night filled with mystery, magic, and more. You won't have to trick them into coming. Just say "Abracadabra!" and watch them appear!

## Magic Mirror Invitations

Magic tricks and illusions often use mirrors to fool the eye. You'll fool your friends when they try to read these invitations. That's because they're written backward! Be sure to tell your guests to hold their invitation up to a mirror and the words will become clear.

*To create your Magic Mirror Invitations, you will need:*

✄ 8½-by-11-inch black construction paper, 1 sheet for 2 invitations
✄ cardboard
✄ pencil
✄ plain white paper
✄ scissors
✄ clear tape or glue stick
✄ mirror

Draw the shape of a magician's top hat onto the cardboard. Cut out the shape to use as a pattern. Fold a piece of black paper in half lengthwise. Trace a top hat on each half and cut out the shapes. Cut a piece of white paper into squares. Tape or glue the square onto the hat. Then write out all your party information backward. Here's how your invitation should look:

ABRACADABRA!

IT'S A SUPER MAGIC SLEEPOVER PARTY!

WHO? _____

WHERE? _____

WHEN? _____

Pickup time next morning _____

Bring your sleeping bag and overnight stuff!

RSVP _____

(Hold this up to a mirror)

## Now-You-See-It Magic Decorations!

Set the mood for magic and mystery in your Abracadabra party room! Create a magic crepe paper streamer tent for tricks, games, and crafts. When it's time to disappear into your sleeping bags and go to sleep, arrange the bags inside the tent.

61

*You will need these items for your Abracadabra party room:*

★ cardboard
★ pencil
★ black poster board
★ string
★ three rolls of black crepe paper
★ three rolls of white crepe paper
★ clear tape
★ scissors
★ hole punch

*Here's how to make your magic streamer tent:*

Cut lengths of streamers long enough to reach from the center of the ceiling to the floor near the walls. Ask an adult to help you attach the streamers to the center of the ceiling with tape. Carefully stretch the streamers to the sides of the room, twisting them as you go. Tape the ends to the floor.

Now draw the shape of a large top hat and a big question mark on the cardboard to use as a pattern. Cut out the shapes. Trace top hats and question marks on the black poster board. Cut them out. Make as many as you like.

Punch a hole in each cutout. Tie strings of different lengths through the holes. Hang your Abracadabra decorations from the ceiling, in the doorways, and at the windows. Keep the lights turned down low for extra effect.

# Say-the-Magic-Word Games!

Your guests have gasped in awe at your magical decorations. Now they're wondering what tricks you have up your sleeve. So dazzle and delight them with these amazing feats of magic party fun!

## Make Your Own Magic Wands

With a wave of this wand, you'll feel magic in the air!

*You will need:*

* black construction paper
* plain white paper
* clear tape

Magicians' magic wands are black with a white tip at one end. Give each of your guests her own supplies and these simple instructions:

Roll the black paper as tightly as you can. Make it as solid and sturdy and possible. Tape the edges of your rolled-up tube in place.

Then cut out a two-inch-wide strip of white paper. Wrap it around one end of the black tube. Tape it in place.

## Magic Wands at Work

Once everyone has a wand, it's time to take turns being a magician. When it's your turn, tap someone with the white tip of your magic wand and give a magic command. Here are some suggestions:

- Poof! You're a chicken. Start clucking!
- Poof! You're an opera singer. Sing like an opera singer!
- Poof! You're a monkey. Act like one!
- Poof! You're a ballerina. Dance!

Now make up some magic commands of your own!

## Magic Messages

Teach your guests the trick of making magic messages appear right before their eyes!

*You will need:*

- white paper
- highlighter pens (any color except yellow)
- regular pens
- white crayons

Before your guests arrive, prepare magic messages for each of them. Use the white crayon to write on the white paper. When it's time to teach the trick, give each guest a message and a highlighter pen. Have them use the highlighter to color the entire piece of paper. They'll be amazed when a magic message appears! Here are some message ideas to get you started:

- You will be rich and famous!
- You will marry a zookeeper and will always have lots of pets!
- You will win a prize for being the *best* best friend!
- You will be a great artist!
- You will find something valuable . . . if you ever clean your closet!
- You win the prize in this magic message game! (Give a prize of an inexpensive magic trick to share.)

## The Incredible Levitating Lift

Here's one trick with no strings attached! Did you ever see a magician make someone's body rise high into the air? You can levitate your arms with this magic trick!

Stand in an open doorway. Let your arms hang loosely at your sides. Then press the backs of your hands against the doorframe. Press as hard as you can. Count slowly up to twenty.

Now step out of the doorway and let your arms drop to your sides. It's very important to relax your arms. In a moment, they should rise up as if being pulled by invisible strings. You and your guests will be amazed!

## The Magic Magnetic Finger

Tell your guests you can make your finger into a magnet—with soap!

Fill a bowl with water. Sprinkle lots of black pepper on top, enough to cover the water surface. Then rub your finger back and forth across a bar of dry soap.

Take *another* finger—one *without* soap on it—and touch the middle of the pepper layer. Nothing will happen. Now touch the pepper with the finger that touched the soap. Abracadabra! A pepper magnet!

## Magic Tapping Tunnel

Make an ordinary coin travel through a magic matchbox tunnel!

*You will need:*

- ♥ small coin
- ♥ pencil
- ♥ small, empty cardboard matchbox

Make sure the matchbox is empty. Now slip the coin into the "tunnel" between the bottom of the sliding drawer and the box cover. Hold the box in one hand. Make sure the coin is at the bottom of the box, near your hand.

With your other hand, take the pencil and tap the top end of the box. Keep tapping sharply. The coin will travel up the tunnel—and appear out the top of the box! How did you do it? It's magic!

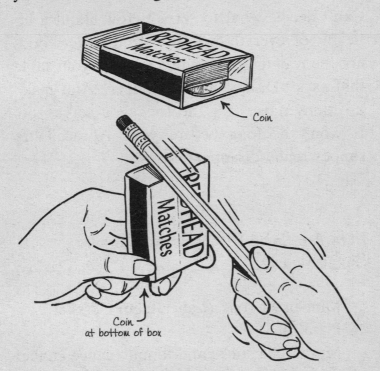

Coin

Coin
at bottom of box

# Abracadabra! Supper Is Served!

Can't decide what to serve? How about a little bit of everything? Bite-sized finger foods are the way to go! Create a sign for your table that says "Disappearing Dinner." And make up funny names for the food you serve, too. It won't be long before your Abracadabra supper really disappears!

## Here Are Some Disappearing Dinner Suggestions:

 Mini–pizza rolls (Label them "Pssssst . . . Pizza!")

Mozzarella sticks and tomato sauce (Label them "Magic Mozzarella Wands")

Mini–egg rolls (Label them 'Razzamatazz Egg Rolls")

Mini–cocktail hot dogs in buns (Label them "Houdini's Disappearing Dogs")

Mini–spinach pies (Label them "Magical Mystery Pies")

70

Celery stuffed with cream cheese (Label them "Vanishing Veggies")

Carrot sticks and ranch dip (Label them "Tricky Sticks and Magic Dip")

Selection of juices in juice boxes (Label them "Magic Potions")

For dessert, offer slices of pound cake with canned peaches on top. Label them "Abracadabra Peach Treats."

## Midnight Snack-in-a-Sack

Can't pull a rabbit out of a hat? Then why not grab snacks from a sack? Decorate brown paper lunch bags. Fill them with secret snacks—a different snack in each bag. Tie the bags closed with ribbons. When snack time comes, let each guest choose a sack and pull out a snack! Trade and share snacks.

*Here are some snack-in-a-sack suggestions:*

- popcorn
- pretzels
- Gummi Bears

- yogurt-covered raisins
- cheese puffs
- mini-marshmallows

### Magical Mystery Breakfast

Your friends will think you're serving every-day, ordinary cereal. Until they find a magical mystery message in the bottom of their bowl! Serve cereal in clear bowls. Serve juice in clear glasses. Before you put anything in the bowls or glasses, tape tiny messages underneath each one. Check each bowl and glass to make sure you can read the messages. The messages should say: Thanks for coming to my Abracadabra Super Magic Sleepover!

# Party 6: Supermodel Makeover Sleepover

Do your friends have a passion for fashion? These makeup, hair styling, and beauty treatments are fit for a princess! Your friends will be model guests at your Supermodel Makeover Sleepover.

### Lipstick Invitations

Your friends will grin at these clever lipstick tube invitations! And they'll know that your party will be as special as your invitation!

*You will need:*

✂ 8½-by-11-inch sheet of yellow construction paper, one for two invitations

✂ 8½-by-11-inch sheet of pink construction paper, one for four invitations
✂ tape
✂ pen

Fold the yellow paper in half lengthwise. Cut so that you have two 4½-inch cards. Tape closed the bottom and side edges of each card. Leave the top edges open. This makes two lipstick tubes.

Now fold the pink paper in quarters. Cut the paper along the folds so you have four rectangular pieces. Hold the pink paper lengthwise. Cut the corners off the tops of the pink pieces to round them off. They should look like lipsticks. Write your party information on the pink lipstick tubes.

Your invitation should say:

Supermodel Makeover Sleepover Party

Come to a beauty-up night at _____'s house.

Address: _____

Date: _____ Time: _____

Pickup time next morning: _____ RSVP _____

Lots of makeover fun for everyone! Bring your hairbrush! Bring your sleeping bag! Bring your overnight stuff! Bring yourself!

Slip one pink paper lipstick inside each yellow lipstick tube. It should look like this:

## SUPERMODEL MAKEOVER SLEEPOVER PARTY!

Come to a beauty-up night
at _____ 's house.
Address: _____
Date: _____ Time: _____
Pickup time next morning: _____
RSVP _____
Lots of makeover fun for everyone!

When the guests arrive, send them straight to the changing room to put on a "dressing gown." (Dad's old shirts are perfect for this!) Then lead them into the beauty salon, where the makeup, hair, and fashion fun will take place. Put out plenty of fashion magazines just like the real beauty salons have.

Set up "beauty stations" for hair, nails, makeup, and fashion. Set up a "fashion design station" for decorating clothes. And a photo shoot area for modeling, too.

*Some ideas for your Hair Station are:*

❀ mirror on a stand
❀ barrettes
❀ scrunchies and hair bands
❀ ribbons
❀ bobby pins
❀ hair spray
❀ styling gel
❀ hair glitter
❀ clean hairbrushes

*Some ideas for your Nail Station are:*


❀ bowl of soapy water for soaking
❀ drying towels
❀ emery boards
❀ cuticle sticks
❀ selection of nail polishes
❀ nail polish remover
❀ cotton balls
❀ nail tattoos
❀ nail jewels


*Some ideas for your Makeup Station are:*


✳ mirror on a stand
✳ eye shadows
✳ eye liner pencils
✳ mascara
✳ blushes
✳ makeup brushes
✳ lipsticks and lip liner pencils
✳ Q-tips
✳ tissues
✳ cotton balls
✳ cold cream for makeup removal

*Some ideas for your Fashion Fun Station are:*

- stick-on earrings
- fake tattoos
- costume jewelry: necklaces, bracelets, rings
- sunglasses
- hats
- scarves

*For your Photo Shoot Area you will need:*

- white sheet hanging on the wall for background
- camera with a flash
- film (plenty!)
- props (shampoo bottle, lipstick, chairs, etc.)

*For your Fashion Design Station you will need:*

- white T-shirt for each guest
  and/or
- white painter's cap for each guest
  and/or
- plain white shoelaces
- colored fabric markers
- glitter glue

## Makeover Fun for Everyone!

Let everyone have fun trying out all kinds of new looks. Have friends take turns helping one another with daring new hair, makeup, nails, and accessories. You might end up with a whole new you!

## Supermodel Photo Shoot

Once you're happy with your Supermodel Makeover look, it's time to do what the supermodels do—pose for pictures! Take turns being the photographer and the model. The photographer arranges all the models in poses.

Set up photo shoots for fashion ads. Before you snap the pictures, decide what each advertisement will be. Will you do a lipstick and makeup advertisement? If so, the photographer should take close-up pictures of the models' faces. Or how about an ad for a new shampoo? Photograph the hair and face only! Or pose the whole group of models together for a full-page fashion spread and let everyone think up her own pose.

Best of all, when your makeover pictures are developed, you'll have great souvenirs of a model sleepover party!

## Be a Fashion Designer

Give your glamorous guests a chance to do some designing of their own! Send them to the Fashion Design Station, where they can make their own T-shirts, caps, and fancy shoelaces. When the fashions have dried completely, your guests can model their latest creations!

# Friends Forever Friendship Rings

No matter how you look on the outside, re-member that it's who you are on the inside that really counts. Celebrate the fact that friends like each other just the way they are with these friendship rings.

*You will need:*

- ❤ seed beads
- ❤ wire twist ties
- ❤ scissors

First, peel the paper off a twist tie. Carefully string the beads onto the wire. Add enough beads to wrap around your finger. Twist the wire ends together to make a ring. Trade rings with a friend and make another for yourself!

# Supermodel Super Supper

Make a sign for your buffet table that says "Supermodel Salad Bar." Give each guest a plate. Then choose from this spread of supermodel favorites:

★ lettuce
★ tomatoes
★ cucumbers
★ shredded carrots
★ celery
★ green peppers
★ macaroni salad
★ fruit salad
★ cheese chunks
★ ham and turkey chunks
★ a selection of salad dressings
★ bread sticks or rolls
★ flavored iced tea

## And for Dessert, Serve Your Guests a Supermodel Mud Pack!

But don't put this mud pack on your face. Eat it! In a baking dish, layer chocolate cookie crumbs, caramel sauce, softened chocolate chip ice cream, and a last layer of chocolate cookie crumbs. Freeze until serving time.

## Makeover Midnight Snacks

You and your friends have new looks. So why not give your midnight snack a new look, too? Grab the old cereals you know so well. Then mix and match them until you find the mixed-up-cereal makeover you like best!

## Roll-Out-of-Bed Roll-up Breakfast

After your beauty sleep, roll out of your sleeping bags and roll up some delicious breakfast burritos!

*You will need:*

- tortillas
- cream cheese
- grape jelly
- walnuts
- toaster oven

With an adult's help, warm the flour tortillas in a toaster oven. Then spread cream cheese, grape jelly, and walnut pieces on the tortilla. Roll them up and eat. Delicious! And when it's time for your guests to get rolling home, thank them for being supermodel guests!

# Michelle's Super Sleepover Party Planning Dos and Don'ts

Great planning is what makes a sleepover party great! My handy planning dos and don'ts will help you have an awesome party from start to finish. DO read the tips and DON'T forget to have a good time!

**1. Do let your parents help plan the party.**
It's your party, but the more help you have in planning it, the better. Start planning your party three weeks ahead of time. Choose the best party date together with your parents. Send out your party invitations two weeks in advance. That gives your friends plenty of notice so they can keep that day free for your party.

Next, talk about the theme, the food, the games, and the party supplies you will need. Divide up the getting-ready jobs. If you let your parents help with invitations, decorations, and party food, you won't be too tired to have fun when party time comes!

## 2. Don't invite too many guests.

At a sleepover, the *less* the merrier seems to be true. Try to invite no more than four or five guests who will get along well. A small group of friends lets you have a cozy time that's fun for all.

## 3. Do be the hostess with the mostest.

You're the hostess of the party. That means it's your job to make sure your guests have a good time. As each friend arrives, give her a warm welcome and tell her how glad you are she could come. Introduce her to your parents. Show her where to put her sleeping bag. Offer her a drink and a snack while you wait for the other guests to arrive.

## 4. Don't spend a lot of money on decorations.

In fact, don't spend any money on decorations! You can find things around the house that will make great decorations. Each party theme has suggestions for decorations using materials you probably already have. If you don't, use your imagination and creativity!

**5. Do explain the house rules to your guests.** When all of your guests have arrived, take a few minutes to explain the rules for the party. Let them know which rooms are off limits and which ones are not. Mention where food may be eaten, where games may be played, when the lights must be turned off, and any other house rules.

**6. Don't forget to tell the guests what time they should be picked up in the morning.** As each guest is dropped off at your house for the party, remind them of the pickup time in the morning. After a night of partying, guests will be tired the next day. Plan to serve breakfast between eight and nine A.M. Your party should officially end around ten A.M. That gives you and your friends plenty of time to catch up on homework, sleep, and family duties.

**7. Do give your guests a tour of your house so they'll feel comfortable sleeping over.**
Comfortable guests are happy guests! Even if your friends have been to your house before, it's a good idea to give them a tour. Show them where you'll all be sleeping. Point out the light switches in hallways. Show them where the bathrooms are. Let them know that there will be night-lights in the hallways, in the bathroom, and in the sleepover room.

**8. Don't forget to remind everyone to brush their teeth after the midnight snacking!**

**9. Do have a separate "sleepy time room" for girls who want to go to bed early.**
As the night wears on, some of your guests will wear out. These sleepyheads will appreciate it if you have a separate "sleepy time room" for anyone who wants to go to bed early. Make it cozy with a night-light and plenty of pillows.

**10. Don't forget to thank everyone for helping to make your sleepover party the best party ever!**

4

# Michelle's List of Lists

Whenever I plan a party I like to keep track of whom I've invited and whether or not they are coming. Here's a list for each party so you can keep track of your guests, too!

Party Theme: _Rugrats_

| Guests Invited | Coming |
| --- | --- |
| Shannon | ___yes ___no |
| Ally | ___yes ___no |
| Rosa | ___yes ___no |
| maggie | ___yes ___no |
| tara | ___yes ___no |
| katy | ___yes ___no |
| Sammy | ___yes ___no |
| Lauren | yes ___no |

89

Party Theme: _____

| Guests Invited | Coming |
|---|---|
| _____ | __yes __no |
| _____ | __yes __no |
| _____ | __yes __no |
| _____ | __yes __no |
| _____ | __yes __no |
| _____ | __yes __no |
| _____ | __yes __no |

Party Theme: _____

| Guests Invited | Coming |
|---|---|
| _____ | __yes __no |
| _____ | __yes __no |
| _____ | __yes __no |
| _____ | __yes __no |
| _____ | __yes __no |
| _____ | __yes __no |
| _____ | __yes __no |

Party Theme: _____

| Guests Invited | Coming |
| --- | --- |
| _____ | __yes __no |
| _____ | __yes __no |
| _____ | __yes __no |
| _____ | __yes __no |
| _____ | __yes __no |
| _____ | __yes __no |
| _____ | __yes __no |

Party Theme: _____

| Guests Invited | Coming |
| --- | --- |
| _____ | __yes __no |
| _____ | __yes __no |
| _____ | __yes __no |
| _____ | __yes __no |
| _____ | __yes __no |
| _____ | __yes __no |
| _____ | __yes __no |

Party Theme: _____

| Guests Invited | Coming |
|---|---|
| _____ | ___yes ___no |
| _____ | ___yes ___no |
| _____ | ___yes ___no |
| _____ | ___yes ___no |
| _____ | ___yes ___no |
| _____ | ___yes ___no |
| _____ | ___yes ___no |

Party Theme: _____

| Guests Invited | Coming |
|---|---|
| _____ | ___yes ___no |
| _____ | ___yes ___no |
| _____ | ___yes ___no |
| _____ | ___yes ___no |
| _____ | ___yes ___no |
| _____ | ___yes ___no |
| _____ | ___yes ___no |

# 5

# A Heap of Sleepover Party Ideas

Now that you've learned how I plan my Super Sleepover parties, you're ready to plan some parties of your own! Here are some more themes to get you started:

★ Treasure Hunt Sleepover
★ Make-a-Movie Sleepover
★ Hawaiian Island Sleepover
★ Around-the-World Sleepover
★ Talent Show Sleepover

★ Bring-a-Book Book Club Sleepover
★ Come-As-You-Are Sleepover
★ Valentine Sleepover
★ Carnival Sleepover

Whatever party you have, I'm sure I'll wish my name were on your guest list!

# 6

## Notes

_____

_____

_____

_____

_____

_____

_____

_____

# FULL HOUSE Stephanie™

| | |
|---|---|
| PHONE CALL FROM A FLAMINGO | 88004-7/$3.99 |
| THE BOY-OH-BOY NEXT DOOR | 88121-3/$3.99 |
| TWIN TROUBLES | 88290-2/$3.99 |
| HIP HOP TILL YOU DROP | 88291-0/$3.99 |
| HERE COMES THE BRAND NEW ME | 89858-2/$3.99 |
| THE SECRET'S OUT | 89859-0/$3.99 |
| DADDY'S NOT-SO-LITTLE GIRL | 89860-4/$3.99 |
| P.S. FRIENDS FOREVER | 89861-2/$3.99 |
| GETTING EVEN WITH THE FLAMINGOES | 52273-6/$3.99 |
| THE DUDE OF MY DREAMS | 52274-4/$3.99 |
| BACK-TO-SCHOOL COOL | 52275-2/$3.99 |
| PICTURE ME FAMOUS | 52276-0/$3.99 |
| TWO-FOR-ONE CHRISTMAS FUN | 53546-3/$3.99 |
| THE BIG FIX-UP MIX-UP | 53547-1/$3.99 |
| TEN WAYS TO WRECK A DATE | 53548-X/$3.99 |
| WISH UPON A VCR | 53549-8/$3.99 |
| DOUBLES OR NOTHING | 56841-8/$3.99 |
| SUGAR AND SPICE ADVICE | 56842-6/$3.99 |
| NEVER TRUST A FLAMINGO | 56843-4/$3.99 |
| THE TRUTH ABOUT BOYS | 00361-5/$3.99 |
| CRAZY ABOUT THE FUTURE | 00362-3/$3.99 |
| MY SECRET ADMIRER | 00363-1/$3.99 |
| BLUE RIBBON CHRISTMAS | 00830-7/$3.99 |
| THE STORY ON OLDER BOYS | 00831-5/$3.99 |
| MY THREE WEEKS AS A SPY | 00832-3/$3.99 |
| NO BUSINESS LIKE SHOW BUSINESS | 01725-X/$3.99 |
| MAIL-ORDER BROTHER | 01726-8/$3.99 |
| TO CHEAT OR NOT TO CHEAT | 01727-6/$3.99 |
| WINNING IS EVERYTHING | 02098-6/$3.99 |
| HELLO BIRTHDAY, GOOD-BYE FRIEND | 02160-5/$3.99 |

It doesn't matter if you live around the corner…
or around the world…
If you are a fan of Mary-Kate and Ashley Olsen,
you should be a member of

# MARY-KATE + ASHLEY'S FUN CLUB™

Here's what you get:
**Our Funzine**™
An autographed color photo
Two black & white individual photos
A full size color poster
An official **Fun Club**™ membership card
A **Fun Club**™ school folder
Two special **Fun Club**™ surprises
A holiday card
**Fun Club**™ collectibles catalog
Plus a **Fun Club**™ box to keep everything in

To join Mary-Kate + Ashley's Fun Club™, fill out the form
below and send it along with

U.S. Residents – $17.00
Canadian Residents – $22 U.S. Funds
International Residents – $27 U.S. Funds

**MARY-KATE + ASHLEY'S FUN CLUB**™
**859 HOLLYWOOD WAY, SUITE 275**
**BURBANK, CA 91505**

NAME: _Samantha Soares_

ADDRESS: _30 Kathleen Dr._

_CITY: _Warren RI_ STATE:_____ ZIP:_____

PHONE:(___) _____ BIRTHDATE:_____

1242

# FULL HOUSE™

# SISTERS

A brand-new series starring Stephanie AND Michelle!

## #1 Two On The Town

Stephanie and Michelle find themselves
in the big city—and in big trouble!

## #2 One Boss Too Many

Stephanie and Michelle think camp will be major fun.
If only these two sisters were getting along!

*When sisters get together...expect the unexpected!*

A MINSTREL® BOOK
Published by Pocket Books

2012-01